Dedication
To parents and educators everywhere
who teach us the importance of environmental
protection and awareness.

To the reader:
My first book, Pirates & Mermaids, took us on
a journey into the imagination, a journey
to the sea. The mermaids celebration was
a result of their successful effort in teaching
littering sea pirates a lesson about polluting our
beautiful oceans.
Pirates and Mermaids(Rivers & Streams) takes a look
at our precious "freshwater" sources. This journey
takes us inland, because everything we do inland
affects our oceans and seas...

The mermaids were celebrating, relaxing in the sun. They had some time off to rejoice and have fun.

The queen of the mermaids told them when they were through, that she had a special mission she would like them to do.

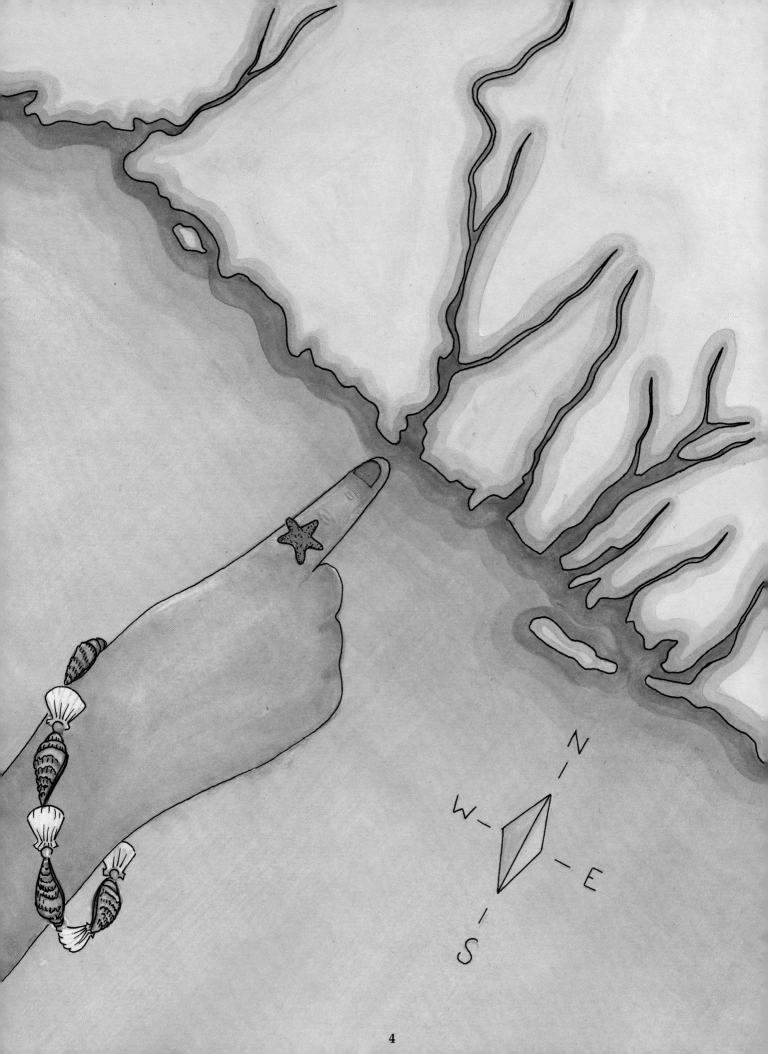

"Our seas are secure!" she said.

"No more naughty pirate schemes.
Now it's time to move inland
to protect our rivers and our streams!
Our freshwater friends heard about
our last stand so they asked us
to join them and give them a hand."

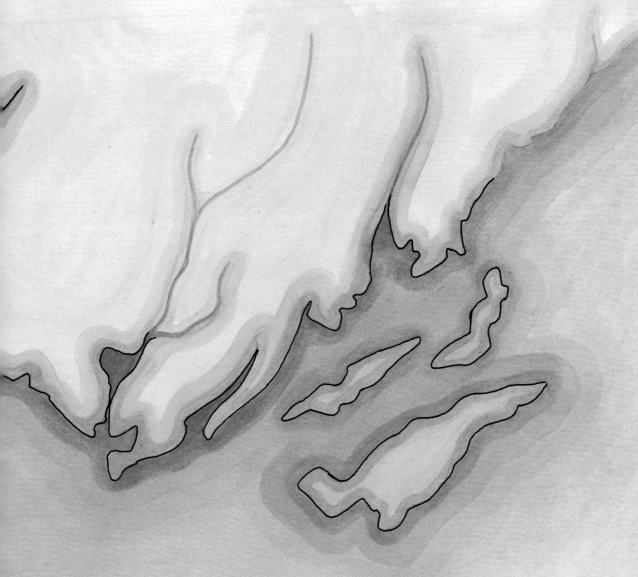

The mermaids had taught the pirates
a lesson on pollution.
Now the river team needed a
freshwater solution.

The sea team swam upriver.
They were the queen's best.
They stopped at a waterfall
to plan and to rest.

Just as they planned, as morningtime rose,
the litterbugs came to the river.

The mermaids giggled and the crabs
snapped their claws since they
had a message to deliver.

The litterbugs were quick.
They didn't waste any time.
They threw trash into the river,
unaware of their crime.

One curious litterbug ran to the river
to see where the rubbish goes.

When he leaned over to take a closer look,

A BLUECRAB LOCKED ON HIS NOSE!

The rest of the litterbugs
scrambled with fear.
They didn't understand why the
blue crabs were there.

They ran and screamed
but had no place to go.

Some jumped into the river
with a crab on each toe.

Once in the river, the litterbugs cried,
The water was dirty and dark.
And just when they thought they
might be safe.
They came face to face with a shark!

But aside from the trash,
they still had pollution
from fluids like gasoline and oil.

These types of pollutants
move quickly in water and
then into our wells and our soil.

The queen needed help to clean
the pollution in the river.
So she recruited a team that she
knew would deliver.

The carp swept the floors;
frogs cleared the ridges.
The trout and the bass helped
with the falls and the bridges.

Then they had an idea
to make power from the trash.
Who said it couldn't be done!?

It was an idea they all knew would work,
just like solar power creates energy from the sun.

The recovery team worked hard;
they wouldn't use the word "can't".

They turned the garbage into electricity
at the trash-to-energy plant.

The queen was excited.
The plan was a success.
This was a tremendous discovery.

The waters were cleaner.
The fish could now smile.
They were leaders in resource recovery.

They *reduced* the pollution,
re-used what they could.
They *recycled* the rest just as
we all should.

The queen gathered all and started to speak.
"EDUCATION!" she said, "is the key.
Be aware that everything we do inland
has effects from the rivers to the sea.
Be kind to the planet,
understand what it's worth.

Awareness will help us protect MOTHER EARTH".

The sea team said goodbye to
their freshwater friends.

The sun on the river was glowing.

The mermaids sang a song that
encircled the earth.

THE MESSAGE WAS:

AWARENESS and KNOWING

The End